# LUK

The moon cast an eerie pale ligh
as Luke trudged his way acro:
faithful dog, Sue, ran on ahead to be
that had covered her belly and flanks. ner snort tan wagged as sne
mounted the bank that divided the start of the mud from the
marsh. Luke looked up from the glutinous expanse in front of him
and gave a glance behind at the estuary and all the water flowing
out to sea. In his hand he held five plump widgeon, two ducks and
three magnificent feathered drakes and reflected on the distance
they had flown in the last week. These were the first of what, he
hoped, would be many this coming winter.

Luke was the youngest son of the local milkman who farmed on
the hills overlooking the large river that drained out into the
English Channel at Boninnich Ferry. He often went wildfowling in
the winter and had mentioned to Mrs Bishop, one of his dad's
regular customers while delivering her three pints of milk a day,
that when he next got a duck he would let her have one.

Now tonight, as the frost set in, he had five birds, three for his
home and a pair for the woman who was not well. Her husband
was the local vicar, and they had a daughter who he had spent more
than a minute glancing at as she busied her pretty little self in the
back of the house, as he collected the week's money from her
mother.

The daughter, Sarah, was always at home on Saturday and
helped her aging but agile father in his church work administering
all the help she could. On Saturday night she sat around the fire
while her father read his sermon for the next day to her. She
helped him find the right words to explain the meaning of the text
better, work out the breaks from reading to look up at the
congregation and help them take note of what he had said.

With her help his half hour of preaching was never dull; her
young brain seemed to add life to each and every word her father
uttered, people came regularly to church to hear what he had to
say. Her love of the natural world and all in it, helped to make his

sermons more real as a fair proportion of the gathered worshippers were farming folk and understood such words.

***

The old dog was sniffing the rough marsh grass as Luke made the safety of hard ground and wiped the mud from his boots. 'Come on Sue,' and started his half- mile walk back to the window-lit farmhouse lying up the slope of the hill.

The fields were white with the frost in the air, even at this low level near the tidal salt water. He buried his left hand into his jacket pocket and with his cold fingers counted the seven cartridges that remained of the twelve he had left home with, five shots and five birds. 'Very good' he mused to himself, was he going to tell dad though that he had missed an easy mallard earlier? 'No' He thought it best not to; he had been fortunate getting two widgeon with one shot and would not say a word. It sounded better; five shots for five kills.

He knew that Mr Bishop had been a fine shot in his younger days and wondered whether to present him with his pair of birds in the feather or pluck them for him. He was a busy man; his wife was ill and the feathers got everywhere, he decided to make a little tied up bunch of the pretty primary and tail feathers instead, something the old man could put in his hatband, and give them the birds ready dressed for the oven.

***

Luke entered the back door and kicked his muddy boots into the porch, then stood his old single barrel in the corner checking again to make sure that it was unloaded, though he knew it was. As he placed the duck on the kitchen table his mother screamed at him to 'wipe the bloody dog down,' it had run into the living room to find the fire and was rolling around on the rug in the excitement of finding the fire alight. He called Sue and gave her a brisk rub down outside the back door with an old sack. Then washing his hands he joined his mum, dad and dog in front of the fire for tea. After they had eaten Luke picked two of the widgeon in the grate throwing the feathers on the fire and left the kitchen at six o clock to start the milking.

2

Early next morning at the vicarage he left the two plump birds with the woman of the house. It took him most of the morning to deliver to the seventy customers his dad's round consisted of. He then had to go home to feed and water the pony and wash down the dray, help bottle tomorrow's milk and load the cart for next day.

His mother churned butter in an old wooden hand tumbler and patted it into lovely round half-pound cakes. Then with a wooden stamp she impressed the word, 'Malpass' into the top and wrapped it in a piece of white paper.

***

Tomorrow, Saturday, was a big day, as not only did he have to drop off the extra milk for Sunday, he also had to collect the weekly amount owed to him. He had few debtors; the odd one would hide on his approach but they always paid him the following week. Things were not always easy for the population in 1939 England; there were rumblings of unrest in Europe, and talk of war.

***

The snow that had fallen in the night had frozen hard as Luke opened the back door that morning, and he shivered, not at the scene before him of a frozen yard but of the thought of the round to come.

His mind was out on the mud flats thinking of all the new arrivals he had heard whistling high overhead as they set their wings to land on the water, tonight would be a good flight, with the chance of a few more birds for dinner.

***

That morning the vicars daughter came to the door of the vicarage and looking at him, said softly in a quite voice.

"Please step in-side; I will get the money. Mummy has it in a tin on the shelf in the kitchen," then she turned and vanished.

Her father had heard the knock and passed his daughter going to the kitchen, as he came to the door to thank Luke for the two duck, saying that his wife had really enjoyed them, but alas was now poorly and in bed. Sarah came to the door and placing the coppers in Luke's hand. He noticed how white her pretty slender

3

hands were compared to his hard rough work tanned palms. She smiled at him and he felt his face blush.

"That's correct," he said as two half crowns followed the coppers in a little pile into his cold large hands. She took his fingers in hers and gave them a long stare feeling his rough callused hand then gave them a squeeze.

"See you next week take care of your hands," he stepped outside noticing as he did so the feathers in her father's hat on the peg in the hall.

Nearly finished now for the day his step to the horse had a new spring to it. Something about the girl did things to him; he thought she could only be about seventeen years old yet she seemed so mature for her age. She had a tender sort of glow that seemed to be contagious. He felt that next week was too long to wait to see her again, so turned in his steps and once again knocked on the front door.

Sarah had obviously not moved from the door as it opened immediately. She had been standing and wondering to herself if he came every morning with the milk. She had not noticed the handsome boy before.

"Sorry," he said as she opened the door. "You overpaid me by a penny," and he offered her a penny.

"Oh you shouldn't have bothered coming back. You could have taken it off next week. I am sorry," secretly knowing to herself that it was a wicked ploy to see her again, had she not counted the money into his huge hand and he not said that's correct, she felt as if her whole body hidden from his eyes beneath her clothes was tingling with excitement, she felt flattered. Never before had her mother made a mistake with the milk money, but she used the excuse that her mother was ill.

"Are you going to the dance tonight?" Luke said in his haste, not wanting Sarah to shut the door and not being ready to speak on any other subject.

"I can't," she said. "My mother is ill, I'm sorry." She now became conscious of the sensation rippling over her, a date with Luke and she had to say no.

Luke turned and the door slammed shut behind him. "Damn," he muttered under his breath, I was too brash and eager, and he thought 'I did not do that very well.'

*** 

That night Luke went to the dance in the church hall as usual and Sarah was there. He could not believe his eyes, as always before her father had been present as the night's entertainment sitting at the door taking the sixpence entrance fee.

"Good evening. I thought you couldn't come."

"I couldn't I usually sit with mother but tonight she is really ill so daddy asked me to take his place to keep an eye on things, he has stayed at home to be by her side."

"I am sorry to hear that," Luke said, and they sat in the doorway taking the coats from the other revellers, drinking lemonade the whole evening and getting to know one another.

*** 

At eleven forty five Luke helped her sweep the floor and lock up. Then summoning up all his courage he asked if he could walk her to the vicarage.

There in the porch to the door that he visited each morning to place the milk, he ventured to put his arm around her and drawing her small body to his kissed her, Sarah made no effort to stop him, her mind had been in a daze all that day, she had dreamed of this moment never daring to stop to believe it would ever happen, she let the sensation flood her senses and her body relaxed taking her arms to enclose his bulk in her gentle warm firm clasp. Sarah was coming of age, a woman's feelings awoke that night, so long suppressed in her by her father and the nuns at school, her dormant feelings now over whelmed her. She had to return that kiss and laying her head to one side buried her face in to Luke's, he responded as she had hoped and the pair made the angles sing.

They made sure that they made no noise for her mother was only feet away above them ill in bed. As careful as they were, they must have made the slightest of noise as they tried to be discreet, for they heard the latch to the door lift, only just having time to release each others bodies before the vicar asked if the night had gone well.

His daughter somehow managed to gather her thoughts together in time to answer, "yes father all well and Luke saw me home isn't that good of him."

The old wise man did not look at the pair as he turned to go back to bed but said that was kind of him, he is a good lad, and a girl could not do any harm finding a man like him. Saying goodnight, they parted but not before arranging to meet the following Saturday when he called for the milk money.

\*\*\*

Luke never went out with his older brother Christopher after one night when he had got in a fight in the local pub. That night Luke had parted the pair of troublemakers and to keep the peace had even settled his brother's large bar bill. Telling the landlord it was the last time he would do it, in future if he let his brother run up a tab, he Luke was not paying? He was fed up bailing his brother out of trouble, the times he had paid the bookmaker to stop him paying those menacing visits to the farm and upsetting mother, it had got to stop. Luke now realised he had other things to think of; his money now was needed for other things. He had a girl who he was madly in love with.

\*\*\*

Every night after work he loaded his dray up for the morning; her home was the only place he wanted to be.

The two would stroll out if dry and plan their life ahead of them

\*\*\*

Luke's Father was not well and had been for the last five years complaining of pains in his chest. Luke's courting with Sarah went from strength to strength; soon he was able to keep her out late without her father minding. They had a spot all of there own down in the lane leading to the river, a spot that no one used at night. There they wooed and Sarah promised never to look at another boy.

\*\*\*

On Easter day as spring was at last starting to come, he asked her father if he could have the hand of his daughter in wedlock.

That day the old vicar cried with delight and his wife passed away in her sleep, happy that in the last year her only child had found the man she wanted.

***

That put the dampers on Luke's plan to ask Sarah to marry him, so he put the day off until after the funeral.

It was the beginning of May before he got down on his knee to ask Sarah if she would marry him. She flung her arms around his neck and they kissed emotionally with the tears running down her cheeks.

"I will! I will!" She was pleading more than agreeing to his proposal! The date was set for July as war was raging in Europe, and Luke feared that his call up papers would soon come.

***

Little did he know that the department, which sent out the buff envelopes, was already processing his? He had no intentions of ignoring them like his coward brother had, his stood up on the mantle piece at home where his mother had placed them on the day the two brothers had fallen out over money and no one had seen or heard from Christopher since.

***

Luke had planned his asking to coincide on Friday so they could both go into town the next day and pick an engagement ring. That was the very day that the letterbox clattered while he was on his rounds collecting the weekly money. His old mother picked up the buff envelope fearing the worst. With her eldest son, Christopher, away and no one knowing his whereabouts, this she knew contained the dreaded news that Luke was expected to help his country in its hour of need. She wiped the tears from her eyes and slowly ambled into the old dimly lit kitchen and placed the fearful news on the table propping it up between the salt and pepper pots. Then she went in search of her husband to tell him they had come.

Now the milk round would have to go along with the cows, they had said long ago that the day would come. The old man was nearly seventy and crippled up with arthritis she herself no spring chicken either.

7

There was no need for Luke to go to war, he could claim to remain at home under the reserved occupation act, but both of them knew his heart was not in cows, the only reason he did what he did was to please them. Their eldest son Christopher was the only one that had ever shown any love for the place, now no one knew of his were a bout's having fled the area on the day his papers arrived and the heavy boys from the bookmakers had shown up, an argument had ensued that involved his parents, that night he had packed his bags and vanished.

*\*\**

On Luke's return home late that morning, he saw the brown envelope on the table jammed between the pepper and salt. He picked it up and opened it as his mother came into the room. She had been crying. Her eldest son had left home and had never contacted the family; now her baby was off to war.

*\*\**

The outlook for Britain looked grim. Taking his mother in his arms, he held her to him and told her not to worry. The war would soon be over and he told her of his plans to marry Sarah and settle down.

"Today," he said, "We are buying the engagement ring."

"Please Luke; don't leave it too long before having children. I so much want a grandchild and there are not many years left in me and your father, please."

"We won't mother, I promise. Sarah and I have spoken of a family and she says she loves kids," and he comforted her, but mother you do understand I must do what I can for my country, what would I tell my children if I dodged the conflict, they would call me, a coward. No mother as much as I would like to stay with those I love I must go.

*\*\**

Luke met Sarah at one pm and they caught the bus into town, arm in arm they wandered the streets of the large town looking in jewellers windows, at last they found the ring they loved.

As he placed it on her finger, she pledged never to look at

another man in her life. Luke did not tell her that his papers had come in the post, as he was afraid of ruining the day. He planned to tell her on Monday after a good night out and let her help her father out on Sunday at church.

\*\*\*

On Monday night with her in his arms down their favourite lane, he told her that the following Monday he would have to report to the Army Centre and would more than likely have to go to war. She sank in his arms and sobbed. Luke told her he was not going for long as every one was talking that the war would be over by Christmas.

That last week passed so quickly. Each night Sarah was left in tears. They planned their whole life and he would be back on leave in a few weeks, she was not to worry.

What with losing her mother, now her beloved it was too much. Could he not tell them he could not go yet and wait until they were wed and had consecrated their love together?

\*\*\*

A week later she stood on the train platform and waved Luke off with the promises that he would soon be back on leave. That summer things were going badly for Britain and the Germans were running amok on the continent.

\*\*\*

Luke was passed fit and he joined a regiment and was sent to Scotland. It could not have been further away from his home if the army had tried. He wrote home in his first letter. He loved Sarah and would soon be back to claim her as his wife. Meanwhile he had joined a section of gunners as that was 'just up his street' he claimed, and it meant that he would be well behind the front line he hoped, lobbing his shells over the heads of his fellow troopers at the enemy.

Luke was not long in training but as his home was the other end of the British Isles he was unable to get home on a twenty-four hour pass so never saw Sarah again. Writing often, they kept in touch.

\*\*\*

The summer was turning to autumn and, along with his mates, Luke was suddenly ordered to pack his bags. They were told to load up in some trucks and the next thing they knew they were on the high seas for foreign lands.

***

No sooner had they landed than they were on the move, the heat was dreadful and their reception was no better. The whole regiment were loaded in lorries, the guns the ship had brought were towed behind them into the desert to defend Tobrook from the advancing Jerries. Luke's hope of not being in the front line vanished before his eyes; now he and his regiment, were all there was between him and defeat for Britain in Africa.

Within days he had settled down in the trenches with his four-inch field gun and mates. The sun burnt you in the day and at night brought frost, something Luke could not fathom.

At home in his part of England frost only came in the winter; here it was common at any time of year. For three days he was busy filling sand bags and making gun pits then just as it was finished, some bigwig made them move a mile further out into the desert. He had little energy or time to write to his darling Sarah and tell her he was in the desert even if he had been allowed to; that was classified information.

***

On the fourth month after having moved goodness how many times all hell broke loose. The Germans made a push and Luke's position was in the thick of it. He remembers a bloody great tank looming out of the dust, stirred up by all the explosions around him. Luke and his mates had no time to reload the gun and train it on the evil contraption, so they did the only thing they could and scrambling out of the pit and Ran! The machine gun bullets kicked sand up around his feet as he ran and ran.

The noise, smoke and bangs were something he had never experienced before and even less been trained for. The four ran for their lives up sand dunes and down the other side with no idea of where they were going, caring even less. Anywhere away from here seemed a good idea at the time.

10

Slowly the noise subsided; they lay exhausted on the rock-strewn sand and rested. Blood was running from a head wound of one of his mates and he complained of a headache.

One look from Luke told him to tell his buddy, it was nothing to worry about, only secretly he knew that a wound that deep in this heat was not going to heal very well without help and they only had what they stood in.

***

Water was the first thing they missed and they had no idea where they were. The occasional explosion echoed around the dunes but gave then no clue as to where it was coming from. The sun set that night and they shivered in the cold.

Next morning they buried their mate who had been shot in the head. Never once did he complain and no one noticed his departure from this world. One of the lads said a prayer, then with thirst driving them they started to head east into the rising sun hoping that their mates had been able to halt the advance and still held the Suez Cannel. This would be the way back to their lines.

***

The three walked all that day in the searing sun and found no clues. If only they had stopped to think before moving, they should have retraced their footprints.

Now a stiff breeze, as hot as a blast furnace, was whipping the sand up and covering their tracks. They had to admit that they were lost. Luke was the only one of his two mates who was used to the open air and knew what the sun could do to your skin. He was also the only one to keep his Army tunic, as the other two dropped them onto the sand rather than carry them.

The very thing that made them strip too soon, was lost as it got dark to be replaced by a sky full of stars, and a chill, before morning frost again returned. Luke and his mates buried themselves in soft sand to try and keep some sort of heat in their bodies and Luke's shirt and tunic made an insulator between his flesh and the sand.

***

The other two got very cold and along with nothing to drink,

11

other than their urine, which they caught in their cupped hands and drank, they had nothing. Their mouths were swollen and their tongues felt as if they would choke them as they were so enlarged.

***

The next morning another of the three lads died in his sleep, half buried in the sand. They did not have the strength to do any more than say goodbye with a salute as neither could speak properly.

***

Day three saw Luke trying to raise his only mate onto his feet.

"Leave me mate, I'll be OK," he said. "I can't go on. You go and get help and then come back for me."

Luke left with a nod of his head as if to say see you later mate and staggered off. They both knew it was the last they would ever see of each other but said nothing. He did not even look back but slogged on across the endless miles of red-hot sand as the sun beat straight down. Luke imagined he was plodding across his beloved estuary back home; the heat shimmering in the distance to him was the vast expanse of the water, the sand the clinging mud.

That day the thought of Sarah at the other end kept his legs moving. The thirst in his throat along with the pain in his head and body was mind-boggling. The mud he now trudged across was a small price to pay for a drink. He even thought he saw his love coming to meet him at one point, only to get disappointed as it emerged to be another dune of unrelenting sand.

The sun was low and he was not sure that he would be able to get up if he fell over, never mind lay down to sleep which his mind was telling him to do. Over the last year back home, he had experienced something like this next day after a late night with his girl while on the milk round.

Then he knew that if he had caught a few minutes sleep, he would not wake up. The horse knew the round as well as him and would stop at the next call. There if he were lucky someone would wake him. It had happened once and he had slept for over an hour.

***

With only an hour to go to sunset, Luke saw them but dismissed them as another figment of his confused head, he trudged on but they would not go away, a long train of camels loaded with parcels and boxes held on by ropes, with men walking alongside. They had seen him long before he saw them but took no notice. The last thing they wanted was anyone to know they ever existed.

Their mission was secret to them only. Luke's persistence of walking without looking at them made them curious and one of the men came over to meet him. Luke still had his shirt on; the Arab saw his insignia and realised he was British and spoke to him.

***

Luke collapsed to wake the following day in an Arab camp, surrounded by camels and men clad in blankets. They sat him up, gave him a drink of water and a date to eat which tasted sweet but he was unable to swallow, instead letting it rest on his tongue. All day he lay in the shade of a date palm and watched as the men loaded and unloaded camels with supplies of war, which he knew were British by the marks on the cases.

He was intrigued to know who his saviours were, then that night as their fire blazed and the sparks sailed up into the heavens, one of the men came over to him and quizzed him as to who he was and where he had come from.

He seemed satisfied with the information Luke gave him and moved away to return with a few more dates like the morning's offerings. These Luke managed to swallow and followed up with a drink of water. He felt better and fell asleep under the blanket they had given him.

***

Next day he was amazed to see a half-track car full of Germans arrive dressed in high ranking uniform and salute the Arab man who greeted them with a Nazi salute. Who were these Arabs with the camels loaded with British weapons talking to the enemy? He felt like getting to his feet and asking.

His thoughts were short lived as a big brown Arab with a nasty look in his eye sat down behind him and discretely held a curved blade of a dagger across his throat. Luke got the message and relaxed, and then the Arab smiled in recognition. In any language a knife to the throat meant only one thing! Do nothing and sit still!

Luke did as bade and looked on. The Arab was impressed and they got talking. For a man far from Britain he spoke good English and told Luke that the only reason they had kept him alive was that they had discussed him and come to the conclusion, that perhaps he could be used to bargain with if the English ever caught them.

If the Germans turned nasty they could do the same, or then kill him anyway, so it was in his own interests to keep quiet and let them get on.

Luke lived with this fear that he could be executed at any moment, if the Germans turned nasty.

\*\*\*

One morning as the light came to the sky Luke took himself off as usual behind a nearby dune to do his morning ablutions. He was doing up the belt of his ragged shorts when he heard the sound of engines. His eyesight had not been playing tricks on him for a long time now since the Arabs had feed him, it had been the thirst and lack of nourishment that made one imaging things that were not there.

\*\*\*

Now before him was a column of British army vehicles speeding along in the valley below between another dune and his sand mountain. Waving his arms in the air, he let his legs run without any control. The army lads in the land rovers and lorries saw this figure half stumbling, half falling down the side of the dune and took no chances.

A quick burst of fire at the man pretending to be one of theirs usually brought the enemy out of cover, but this time Luke either fell as his body over toppled his legs in his haste down the shifting sands in his weakened state, or dived for cover. He has no recollection of either; he cannot remember the man even pointing and prodding him with a rifle. His shirt, now only a thread of what he was issued with, still had his insignia on it and this alone saved him again.

\*\*\*

The fact that his dehydrated body was gaunt and sun burnt, led

14

one to see that this man had once been a strong fellow and again, with water and food, he could be a force to reckon with.

The group agreed to take him along with them for now and gave him water.

His first recollection is next day as one of the group sat him up and gave him water. All he could tell them is of the day he had been taken pity on by a caravan of Arab gun runners and only kept alive on the merest rations; how long he had been in their custody he had no idea.

At first he had placed a small stone in his shorts pocket each day, to record the passage of the days, but the heat had muddled his head and he could never by noon remember whether he had or had not picked one up, so soon lost count.

***

Back home in England that very day that Luke was eventually picked up by his country's own soldiers, his father passed away from a heart attack. The news that his son was reported missing in action so long ago now, with no more news was too much for the tired old man.

His mother was devastated; now she was alone. If it were not for the frequent visits from Sarah, she would easily have gone to bed and lay there until she too joined her family on the other side. She was sure Luke would have been there to greet her like he had his father at the gates.

***

The farm was now nothing but rough grazing for the sheep, whose owner paid her a pittance each year. Sarah came to the house every evening and sat with her. Often the two women just sat and listened to the birds of the estuary flying over the roof, or as they did in the summer, sit and gaze across the vast expanse of brown mud or blue water, depending on the state of the tide. Sarah helped Luke's mother arrange the funeral and her father, now frail and missing his wife, conducted the service.

***

Spring was in the air and it was a lovely day. Sarah never gave up hope that Luke was still alive and remarked how warm it was

15

and said she hoped that it was warm and as pleasant wherever he was.

***

He, far away, was struggling to stay alive in the heat. Later as his strength returned, he told the men who had rescued him that he and three mates had deserted their gun under enemy fire. A court order offence, and he was sorry. The leader of the group listened to his story and then turned to his men and said, "he'll do, he's one of us. All doubts that he was a spy left their heads.

They told him that he was now in the company of a long-range desert patrol and they were 'Top Secret' so no way, could they let his old regiment know he was safe and 'no; he could not even write home'.

As far as the outside world knew, he would stay posted as missing, and that was how it would have to remain until the war was over. Their group was not officially recognised by the War Department; all they did was collect intelligence and sabotage the enemy. It was a new secret set up and that was how it had to remain.

***

Luke's knowledge of field guns was no help to him or them, so he learned to set explosives with fuses on fuel dumps, to go off after they had fled without the Germans seeing them, how to kill a man with a knife silently and disappear.

They were self contained; everything they required, food, fuel, ammo and water, they carried with them, never using their radio in case the enemy got a fix on them. When they left base they vanished, no one in the army knew of their assistance, other than the top brass.

***

They traversed the sands with compass and what knowledge they had. The maps they had were at times useless; many of them were old and the terrain had never been surveyed and anyway the dunes were forever moving with the wind. They had a chap with them who made his own maps as they went along.

Many times the convoy of three jeeps and lorry got stuck and

16

they spent many hours digging, pulling and pushing their vehicles out from the soft sand. Sometimes the going was rough with large stones that punctured their tyres, and one man spent an hour or two each day patching up the tubes, and then laboriously filling them up with air, a thankless job in the heat.

*\*\**

When they did return to base Luke was kept under close guard, to make sure he did not talk or meet anyone as he often spoke of Sarah and his family and how he was sure after all this time of no news from him they would think he was dead.

He felt like a prisoner in his own country, hundreds of his fellow comrades all dressed in Khaki. His mates keep him hidden beneath an old Arab's blanket with only his eyes showing from a slit in his headgear. Soon to be back in the desert as the men collected all their requirements from stores and delivered their information on the enemy's positions. Then one day it all changed.

*\*\**

He was told he had got to shave the growth from his face and cut his hair to report along with the group's leader to his commander. Luke's time in the army told him that an order like that meant something important.

*\*\**

Along with his boss he was taken to the buildings, he had only ever been allowed to see from a distant that the party had collected their provisions from.

The door opened; the two marched in and saluted the officer in the room.

"Take a chair. We do not stand on ceremony here," he said. He then turned to pull the blind of split bamboo down over the window to give them privacy and stop the two from squinting to see him in the glare of the sun streaming through the glass.

"I understand," he stated addressing Luke, "from your commanding officer that you are the one found last year out in the sands."

Luke's startled facial expression made the officer stop to ask if he was OK.

"Yes sir I'm fine, only was it really a year ago? I had no idea; one day was so the same. I tried to keep count when with the Arabs by putting a small stones in my pocket but eventually gave up as I could not remember if I had put one in or not. If sir, it is that long ago, may I know today's date?"

"Certainly young man that's no secret."

The answer shocked Luke. He was eight months older than he thought; his twentieth birthday had gone and he never realised it.

The commanding officer congratulated him and told them both that for a birthday present, they could now expect to be moved as the tour of duty had come to an end, also Luke's parents would be informed immediately that he was no longer posted as missing. There was now a more pressing engagement for them, as they would soon find out, but first all Luke's details were taken and written down so that the War Office back in London could notify his next of kin and remove him from the missing list.

"Congratulations again on your twentieth birthday."

***

Back in the UK, down in Cornwall, the funeral was taking place of Luke's mother. She had lived for the last year a widow. Luke's mother had died of a broken heart. First her eldest son, Christopher, had argued and run up debts all over the place, mainly in betting shops and public houses, then left home after a row with Luke. No-one had seen him since.

Next Luke's call-up papers arrived and later the subsequent 'Missing in Action' letter that had driven her husband into a state to think that within a year he had lost both his sons. Mother had never given up hope and she and Sarah had often sat into the late evening praying and hoping for news.

Sarah's father died one month after Luke's mother, a dried up man who only had his faith to keep him going. He had been so thrilled with Sarah's news that she was to wed and he her father could perform the marriage service.

The news of Luke's loss had been a shock to the whole village. Luke's mother had sold the cows on her husband's death and the land had stood idle for over a year. The ministry of Agriculture was not interested in it as the land was so poor and the hill sheep from next door grazed it.

Now with her death the farm lay forlorn with no knowledge of the were about of the new owner. The son it was left to was nowhere to be found.

* * *

Then one day the eldest one had shown him self and finding the house deserted, had gone to the village to enquire why. It was late in the day and the post office was shut, so not knowing who to seek information from, he had gone to the church and was met by Sarah as she was leaving having spent the last hour on her knees praying for Luke to be safe.

She was pleased to see him, and they took a seat by the door and talked, she brought him up to date on all the news of the village. She asked why he had not come to his mother's funeral and he informed her that he only knew when he had read in the newspaper that his mother had died.

He asked her how her parents were and she told him that they had both died and now lay outside the church door together near his mother, also her love, his brother, was missing in action, he told her it was his own fault he did not have to go.

This hurt Sarah deeply, he was the coward that had run on the first hint of danger, and to her knowledge his danger had only been a debt.

"You live alone in the house then," he said.

"Goodness gracious no!" she said. "I am in digs and hate it." She looked at him and in the glow from the candles lighting the church, she could see the likeness in him of his brother Luke, now dead in her mind, in a far off land.

No gravestone would ever be erected to mark his passing, nowhere for Sarah to go and grieve. Christopher smiled. 'If only,' she thought, 'it could be him.' She was very lonely and very, very vulnerable and Christopher knew it. He put his arms around her and cuddled her in his embrace.

"Sarah; you know he is never coming back. Don't torture yourself."

19

He ran his hands up and down her delicate back and he knew she was responding to his charms. That night he stayed at the room with Sarah and talked late into the night, it was dark in her poky little room; she needed assurance and he was the one tonight to give it to her.

He knew a lot about Luke and told her things that they had done when young. Sarah wanted to know all there was, but he told her only what he wanted her to hear; she was enchanted. Here was Luke in a different body. Why not? Luke was gone.

***

The next day Sarah left the little village she was born in to move up country and live with Luke's brother. Funnily she thought that by going with Christopher she at least would have something of Luke's to remember him by, other than the ring on her finger.

Word spread like wildfire around the village that Sarah had gone from them she was a much-loved girl and to go with a no hoper like Luke's brother beat them all.

***

The new milkman spread the talk faster than anyone. He had known the family all his life. His son had knocked around with Christopher and given him up as a mate the night after he had hit a girl so hard she needed medical treatment to recover. He was a wicked sod to his women he said, especially after a few drinks.

Why Sarah had gone away with him was a mystery to him and he sowed the doubt in all their minds had she voluntarily gone off with him and did anyone see them together before or even on the day? No one could answer that; no one had seen them together. For years the landlady told the story first, as she held up a note in the post office, that read,

'I am leaving with Luke's brother Christopher. Sorry, love Sarah Bishop'

***

The pair in fact had left the village before daybreak on Christopher's motorbike combination, her sitting in the sidecar with her suitcase propped up behind her with all her worldly goods inside it.

As they left the village she nervously fingered her Holy Bible on her lap and twisted her engagement ring around on her finger, as they passed the entrance to Luke's old home she gave the gatepost a last longing glance. She wondered if she was doing the right thing. It was a very impulsive thing she was doing, not like her at all, but she had no one else in the world now her parents were dead, and Luke had gone forever.

***

It was over three and a half years now since that letter had come asking him to enlist and nearly three had passed since his mother had cried while telling her of the news that he was missing. He would never come now so why not Christopher? There was no other boy interested in her.

***

They headed for London and the East End, to a very bombed out place where Christopher lived with a couple of his mates. It was his intention to get her to do all the work around the house for him and his drinking friends.

She was trapped; a young woman of twenty in London living in one of the remaining slums. Hitler's bombs were new to her hidden away in the part of England like she had been; there seldom had war show its ugly head. The shortage in the rations and the stories in the newspapers were all they had known.

***

She soon got used to struggling with the work but the thought of Luke was never far away and every uniform she now saw made her look twice. Was it Luke? Had he lost his memory and no one knew him?

The fear that she had done the wrong thing haunted her every waking hour. Her relationship with Chris was nothing like he had said it would be. Each night he was out and she sat on her own in the candlelight and cried. She even thought about going back to the village by the estuary but so many questions would be asked and she was ashamed of herself. Every time he came home drunk he beat her up, as if a punishment for letting himself get in such a state, and each time she forgave him as he grovelled the following

21

morning asking for her forgiveness.

"It will never happen again," he always promised but it always did.

***

The gossip in the village to the west at last died down and unknown to Christopher he inherited the farm, but the times were hard, to trace the where about of folk as they were bombed out and moved, and a person like him did not encourage the law to know his where off. Sarah Bishop was forgotten another tragedy of the war. Her name was seldom mentioned, and then only after a church service when her father's name came up, as one of the best vicars the parish had ever had.

***

Christopher's life was never dull; he was heavily into the black market, trading in anything he could lay his hands on at a fair price. Sarah saw none of the money, not even a pair of silk stockings that he had a hundred pair of one week.

He gave her a pittance to keep herself alive and ate most of his meals out in pubs or with his friends somewhere. The police were always round her place and it made her feel like the criminal. She had never done a dishonest thing in her life; she felt that God was judging her for forgetting Luke's memory so soon.

***

Many of the women she spoke to had not heard from their men folk for a long time but they stayed faithful, living in hope that one day, just one day, news would come. Sarah consoled herself that none of them had had a letter saying missing and not heard a thing since, all the ones she met, who had got one, sooner or later received a letter from their loved one to say, am now safe as a prisoner.

Some even hoped that the dreaded telegram would flutter onto their doormat telling them their beloved had been killed in action and Sarah thought that that was wicked.

Yet what had she done, at the very first chance, she had slipped away in the darkness leaving only a brief note?

***

The news came to Luke that the camp that they were in was to pack everything up; they were on the move. Where to they had no idea, but the consensus among the other troops, was that as long as it was away from the bloody sand and heat, they didn't care. They were to eat their words within six weeks as the steaming jungle closed in around them, they could not see more than ten yards ahead of themselves for the green foliage of the jungle, this was nothing like the desert.

Instead of flies, which they still had, there were now also leeches, snakes, spiders and ants and to compound all that, swamps and mud. But most deadly of all were the enemy. These tiny little men who they had been told were useless at fighting and would be out of the war in weeks.

*\*\**

Now years later with their conquest of most of the Pacific to the east and a part of China, they were proving a formidable force. They were specialist in booby traps, putting trip wires across the jungle paths, not caring about the locals who got blown up or maimed.

They were terrible, more like animals. To die in battle was to them a glory and brought honour to the family. Stories passed around the campfire, when they dared to light one, of the things they did to any prisoners.

*\*\**

The local population of natives lived in fear of retribution and Luke's mates kept well clear of any known places, for the Japs tortured the native people to tell them of their whereabouts. Luke's party had similar orders to the ones they had in the desert, to vanish into the interior, cause as much damage and collect all the information they could. Their supplies again they had to carry with them.

In these conditions Mules, which could be very stubborn at times, were substituted for the jeeps. Luke's mates had marched from India into Burma and now their only link with civilisation was the temperamental radio sets that they used as little as possible, in case the enemy got a fix on them. With the sets they relayed the information and ordered an airdrop for supplies.

\*\*\*

These were flown over the mountain range from India into Burma by brave pilots in Dakotas, some times through terrible weather and many pilots with crews were lost. A round trip through the most appalling weather of over a thousand miles. Then to find a gap in the forest that the 'Shindigs,' as Luke's mates were called, had cut out of the virgin woodland and drop there cargo to them.

\*\*\*

Luke made a friend in the ranks called Jock; a small well built man from Scotland with a deep accent. Who like Luke had the knack with animals of the horse breed? And each was in charge of a mule that carried their precious supplies. They had two other things in common; number one was to get home and for the F----ng war to end but the thing they talked about most was the duck shooting they loved. The Scotsman shot the Clyde.

He recalled the nights he crouched out on the mud awaiting the duck watching the ships sail by in the darkness and wondering where they were bound, never realising that there were places like the desert or jungle they now found themselves in.

\*\*\*

As it was getting light one day, the call came for them to move on. Luke took up his usual position behind Jock at the end of the line a place most feared and called the tail end Charlie.

No one ever volunteered for the place as any lurking Jap could jump out on you and garrotte you before you had the chance to utter a word. The last end Charlie was privileged the others thought, as you never had to contend with an ass, you needed both hands free in case a Jap did show himself, and you needed to fire quick before he got a shot off.

The trail today led across a ravine and over a nasty leech infested river where they would be exposed to any watching Jap. As they neared the river Luke held back a few yards to watch behind as his mates struggled to get the animals across loaded with ammo.

They hated swimming as much as the men hated wading up to their chins holding their only means of defiance above their heads to keep their rifle dry.

They were all nearly over when Luke spotted a movement up in a tall tree thirty yards away in front of him. A thin barrel moved taking aim at Jock who the sniper had thought was the last man.

***

Jock turned, as he dived for cover, to see who had shot who, only to notice the dead body falling from the tree. There was no noise or panic; everyone took cover and it was a few minutes before the leader gave the signal to move on.

Luke got up from the soggy jungle floor where he had flung himself, ran to the river and waded across in record time under the guns of his mates awaiting the sniper's friends to open up. Nothing happened; he was a lone Jap and they blessed the fact! Jock held his hand out to pull Luke up the bank and gave him a slap on the back.

"If it had not been for you," he said, "I would now be dead and that would never do! Mate, I owe you my life and if ever there is anything I can do to repay you, don't forget to ask."

***

For the next six months Jock never let Luke forget the fact that he owed his life to him, for the Jap snipers were renowned for never missing. The war was coming to a close and all the troops were looking forward to going back to blighty.

Christopher was still up to his old tricks but now he was branching out, so the other ladies in the street had informed her. For some silly reason Sarah was now his wife, in a fit of thinking that the simple act of marrying him, she could change the brute he was. Everyone knew of his nocturnal activities and the local police kept an eye on him, even down to raiding his house looking for stolen goods. Chris was far too shrewd for that, never having had his collar felt.

Now he was getting greedy. The black market was not as lucrative now the Yanks had left for the continent, and finished Hitler off. The boys he mixed and drank with were real rebels and thought nothing of robbery. Christopher spent hours in the back room of a pub planning and plotting this and that, until one of the gang saw a snag, and they had to drop the whole idea as impossible. Then he would go home and take his frustration out on Sarah.

The slamming shut of the back door used to make her freeze for she could tell by the way he moved across the kitchen floor what to expect as she lay in her bed. How she longed to have a bed of her own away from a man like him.

If the mode took him he would rape her or beat her black and blue. Luke's face came to her in those moments; she remembered all those nights down that lane leading to the river and cursed him for getting killed.

She lay in between the blankets at night and prayed that Christopher would not come home tonight, twisting the engagement ring round and round on her finger and listening out for the door. London was slowly coming back to something like normal with fewer hold ups, unlike the days of the Blitz. Now only the unexploded bombs caused disruption as they were dug up.

\*\*\*

Luke and his mates at last came out of the jungle and were told that they would be going home when transport could be arranged. Meanwhile there was a lot to do and volunteers were called for to help get the liberated country cleaned up and running again.

There were prisoners to be repatriated, building work to be done and a lot of junk to be cleared up just to make it safe to live in. The

Japs left many lethal booby traps behind and the odd group of soldiers had not, or would not, except defeat.

Jock had no ties back in Britain and saw no reason to hurry home. He was one of the first to step forward and offer his services.

He said goodbye to Luke and promised to keep in touch. "If you ever want me, you let me know, I owe you my life," were his parting words.

Luke watched him go from the stockade they were staying in awaiting a voyage home.

For the past five weeks now he had been writing home to his mother and Sarah, sitting for hours composing each letter word, by word, explaining why he had not written for years.

Unknown to Luke his letters were piling up behind his front door back home, unopened. The ones to Sarah were being sent back to the War Office as 'Undelivered, Return to Sender' but owing to lack of cargo space, the mail was not being given the priority as usual. The chances now were that he would be home before the letter he was writing reached its destination.

\*\*\*

His ship came in a fortnight before Christmas and left on Boxing Day. He was coming home. He had been gone from England forty-nine days short of five years, five long, hard dangerous years without his love Sarah. It was the thought of her that had kept him going many times. Luke had long ago lost all interest in counting days or weeks so had no idea how long it took before his ship docked in Liverpool.

By now the land had been free of war for nearly two years and there was no welcoming party to greet him, the conquering hero. He belonged to the forgotten army.

\*\*\*

He had written his last letter telling Sarah he would be home soon and had fancifully hoped that she would be there to greet him. A forlorn hope as the very ship he was on carried his letter in its hold and he had not been able to tell her the day the boat would dock anyway.

Luke, like the others, was marched off to an Army camp to be demobbed.

*\*\**

Two weeks later the train drew up at the station he had left five years previously. Sarah was not there so he caught the next bus, which would drop him off near home. From the end of the lane he walked the two miles to his little village and home.

The lane up to his house looked very untidy. Grass and weeds grew everywhere and as he got nearer, it dawned on him that the place looked deserted. He walked around the house; having laid his small cardboard case he had been given down that now held all he owned, and stared in through the kitchen window. The place was empty; across the room he could see the front door and the pile of letters on the floor. No cows grazed the fields as they had when he left.

Where were his mother and father? He needed answers so gathering up his little case he trudged back down the lane to the village. He entered the post office where he was instantly known.

*\*\**

"Luke, my boy! How are you? So nice to see you again."

Luke asked after his parents, the woman came out from behind the counter and took him in her arms, a tear wandered down her cheek, she gently told him that they had both died. His father had a heart attack in 1941 and his mother died of a broken heart a year later, having lost her husband and as she thought, her two sons. There had been little mail from him even though she had written to him weekly until he had been posted missing, then nothing. Where had he been and why did he not write?

Luke was too upset to try and explain to a strange woman. She had no idea of what war was really like, living here in a quiet little village far from it all. He left for the vicarage to see his love but his knock on the door only brought a strange man wearing a dog collar.

*\*\**

"Can I be of assistance my boy?" he greeted him.

"I'm looking for Miss Sarah Bishop," Luke said.

"I'm sorry; she no longer lives here."

"Do you know where she is?"

28

"No sorry; she left when her father died last year. You could try the post office; they may know."

Luke thanked him and turned to retrace his steps. The lady behind the post office counter smiled as he entered.

"Sorry Luke; I was rather off with you earlier. It must have been hell for you. I know you would have written if you could, but I'm afraid we all thought you were dead. Poor Sarah was beside herself with grief, so was her father, God rest his soul. You do not know do you, he passed away and is laid to rest beside his wife, near your mother in the churchyard?

"Yes, I have just come from the vicarage; and Sarah? Do you know where she is? I must see her."

"I'm afraid I don't. The last address I had for her was at Mrs Howlet's, but that was years ago. I believe she lived in digs there for she had to move out of the vicarage when her father died." The poor post woman did not have the heart to tell him that the story was she had fled the village with his brother

\*\*\*

Luke lost no time in getting down the hill to the house he used to deliver milk to. He knocked on the door and after what seemed like an eternity, a frail old lady opened it. She may have had problems answering the door quickly, but there was nothing wrong with her eyesight.

"Luke! What a blessing. We all thought you had been lost forever. Sarah was so heartbroken."

"Is she at home? Only I hear she lives here."

"Oh Luke! She left years ago with your brother. Most odd really, she just upped and went. She never even said goodbye. One day she was here, the next she left a note saying sorry she had to go, left her rent so owed me nothing, but I had a funny feeling that something was wrong. It wasn't like her to do a thing like that. We were real friends; she would sit and chat with me until late in the night, always playing with your ring on her finger. She really loves you my boy, you must find her!"

\*\*\*

The next day saw Luke in the fishing town of Brixham looking for a clue to his love, but after a fruitless search, he had to find a job to keep himself alive. The only thing he could find was a berth on a trawler. At least it was better than an indoor job for he hated to be closed in anywhere.

Luke took to the life of a fisherman as if he had been born to the sea. In any spare time he searched for Sarah. He even visited all the churches in the West Country area hoping to find Sarah in case she had died or had married as a lot of people had said she might have done, thinking he was dead. He looked at all the Sarah's and their new surnames starting with ABC but had to admit defeat as in the last few years there had been many.

Meanwhile the year slipped by and the war memorials started to go up for all those who had fallen in the latest conflict.

***

A month later Sarah, who although now married to his brother, had saved enough money to buy a train ticket to return to her birth place to go to see her true love's name on the new memorial. Her love for Luke still burned inside her, and she was very upset to notice that on the magnificent stone memorial now standing in the churchyard where her mother and father lay, along with Luke's parents, his name was missing.

She ran her fingers down the brass letters of all the fallen to make sure that she had not missed his name in her excitement, but no his name was not recorded there.

Sarah was upset and on returning home wrote to the War Graves Commission to tell them of their error.

To her astonishment she got a very polite letter back, informing her that Luke was still alive and had joined another regiment sometime in the war; however they were not at liberty to disclose the said unit, as it was classified information.

To Sarah this reply came as a real bombshell. She had married his brother in the belief that it would be the closest she would ever come to her true love, Luke.

Now he was alive and she was married to someone she did not love. Her husband had not changed his ways as he said he would, still staying out late at night, drinking, gambling and, for all she

30

knew, having affairs. She had to find Luke and made it her passion looking for any news. She reasoned that maybe he would arrive home to find everyone he loved gone, but it was a start so she wrote a note to the post office in his village asking if there was any news.

***

The woman sent a letter to Sarah by return post saying he had returned, but as there was now nothing for him there, he had left. She didn't know where he had gone. The trail went cold.

Sarah wrote to his old regiment hoping to get an explanation as to where he was and which regiment he had joined. The reply stated that he had transferred to another unit unconnected to theirs late in 1943 but they had no information other than that.

A letter had been sent to his home address informing the next of kin of his reappearance after being posted missing, but it was returned saying 'not delivered'. He was sorry that he had nothing else to report, but there was a reunion coming up of his old company and just maybe someone there could help as they may have seen him. The officer was sorry he could not be of help and wished her good luck in her search.

***

The reunion was scheduled for the coming March and Sarah travelled to the town in question to visit, hoping to get some kind of news of her sweetheart whose ring she still wore alongside the gold wedding ring; she was now three months pregnant with his brother's child.

She approached the hall; a commissionaire greeted her and opened the door for her. The interior of the vast hall was full of men and standing at the furthest corner was a little Scottish man in a kilt. He was talking to a most upright handsome man she had ever seen.

It was her Luke!

Her legs felt like jelly; her heart raced. She must have visibly shaken as the attendant on the door asked if she was all right.

"All right?" she said. "My boyfriend! We all thought that he was dead and there he is, standing there as large as life. Look!"

The attendant stared into the room of over two hundred men,

31

not knowing which one he was supposed to be looking at.

"It is happening all the time, husbands have returned to find their wives are married to others. It's happening all the time love," he said, putting his arm on her shoulder.

"What am I going to do?" she said.

"Go and speak to him, tell him."

She stood in the doorway for ten minutes debating with her conscience as to what she should do. Her heart told her eventually that she had to confront him, and confess her love for him.

She steadily advanced on Luke, as he lay propped up by his arm on the mantelpiece talking to his mate who he had not seen for over eighteen months. They were discussing what they were going to do now that the fighting had ended. Jock had plans; he was immigrating to Canada this next week. Why did Luke not come also? There was potential out in that huge country now that war was a thing of the past.

***

She approached with caution. What if after all these years he did not recognise her? She had changed her hairstyle years ago to be able to keep it dark in the war because there was soot and brick dust everywhere and a shortage of soap. Now today she had a nasty black eye, acquired a few days before. Her belly had butterflies as she neared him. His stature standing there was more stunning than she remembered. Christopher was not the half of him. Her heart ached if only she had waited, as she had promised. All that hurt she had suffered at the hands of Christopher would never have been. Even now she had no idea if Luke would forgive her; even if he did, she was now married and she felt a traitor even to approach him, pregnant by his brother.

Luke was deep in conversation as she stood behind him imagining what it would be like to feel him in her arms. Jock, the Scotch lad Luke was talking to, brought the girl's presence to his notice.

"I believe you have an admirer standing behind you mate."

Luke turned and dropped his glass on the floor, scattering broken glass and the ale over his trousers. Sarah and Luke flung their arms around each other.  Sarah's heart beat twice as fast as his face bent to kiss her.

"No Luke, she said pushing him away from her, I am married."

The reaction to those words even made Jock nearly drop his whisky but being a Scot and having paid for it, he meanly clenched his fist that tight that any other glass would have exploded.

"Christ Luke!  This the lass you have been going on about all these years?"

Luke put his arm around Sarah and pulled her to his side.

"Sarah; tell me what happened to you.  My mother and father; your father?  There is so much missing in my life.

*** 

The three of them left the hall full of noise and sought a restaurant in town so that they could talk quietly.  Jock was a large part of Luke's life and they insisted that he come along with them.  He was only too pleased, as he was hungry.

Over the meal Sarah told all she knew, of home and about how Chris had appeared one day and she had foolishly gone away with him.  Now she longed to be free, not only of him, but the life she was trapped in.  Jock sat silently listening and did not mutter a word until they had finished eating and were all enjoying a smoke.

"Sarah; you must give me your address," he said, "this week I leave for Canada, you say Christopher looks like Luke and drinks every night, a bit like me," giving Sarah the widest of grins.  "I like a good drink and if ever in London would love to meet you again."

Sarah wrote her address down for the pair of them and Luke noticed the careful way Jock folded the paper and tucked it in his jacket's inside pocket along with his wallet.  Luke read his bit of paper and confirmed the address to his memory.

Now he had found his Sarah, he did not ever want to lose her again.  Jock told Sarah how Luke had always spoken of her and the things they had done, even down to the point of calling Luke a hero

"If it was not for him I would not be here now; that right Luke?"

But Luke's mind was far away down a country lane six years ago with a girl in his arms and the sound of her voice, I shall always wait for you rang in his ears."

"Who did you marry Sarah?" he asked, as she turned to look at him after studying the red hair of Jock's head.

"Luke, forgive me please. I married your brother. I thought you were never coming back and he was the closest thing I could do to get near your memory. I now know it was a stupid thing to do; it was done on the spur of the moment. He arrived one day in the village and we got talking. Next thing, I had left with him in the middle of the night, telling no one of my plans. He promised to love me; he can be so persuasive when he wants to be, but in reality he is a bully, liar and a thief. Every night he is out with his so-called mates getting drunk, then on his return home he takes it out on me. But what can I do? I am married for God's sake and now expecting his kid!" Sarah was near to tears and Jock looked on as Luke put his arm around her.

"There is not a lot we can do said Luke but where do you live Sarah?"

"In London, in the East End, near the Elephant and Castle. It is a rough area, all Dockers. They fight in the streets all the time and over nothing usually. Christopher is always coming home bragging about who he hit, and how his victim collapsed after a fist full of his knuckle duster."

***

"A fine block that husband of yours sounds," said Jock. "He needs a good seeing to if you ask me."

"No-one is asking you," Sarah said and Jock's manner showed as he lost interest in a good punch up, especially as the chap seemed to be the right candidate for a thump.

"Christopher has not changed then," said Luke. "He still owes me a small fortune from when I paid his bills at home."

"Change?" said Sarah. "He has got worse. I really don't know what I saw in him. I think I was upset over losing you then he came on the scene and promised the earth." She started to shed a tear, which ran down her bruised cheek. Luke wiped it off with a dab of his top pocket-handkerchief.

"Did he do that?" he asked as Sarah flinched.

"Of course."

***

Sarah had been in Luke's company for nearly an hour when she had to leave to catch the train back to London. A young army lad had offered to run her to the station in his car on his way home. Luke said goodbye out in the street and gave Sarah his address, 'just in case she ever needed to find him,' he told her. He watched her vanish around the corner of the street and then took himself inside to join his mate.

Jock was now not alone, having met another of their old friends from Burma. Luke arrived as they were talking about him and his love, Sarah, and how she had got mixed up with his no good brother. They talked it over for an hour, all the time getting more intoxicated. The general opinion was that nothing could be done, but Jock had his own opinion and kept quiet. The night came to a close and they staggered back to their own digs.

***

Sarah arrived back home in the dark to a very untidy house and she was tired. While Sarah had been away, her husband had had the lads around and planned the perfect break in, which had taken place that night. The proceeds had been taken to his house and divided up.

The washing up they left in the sink for Sarah to do on her return, along with all the mess in the other rooms. Her husband was lying fast asleep and fully clothed on the bed. He was not too happy when Sarah woke him up to find out what had been going on in her absence.

"Nothing to do with you," he said.

It so upset Sarah after the recent events with his brother that without thinking she said,

"Your brother would not treat a dog the way you treat me."

She had not told him where she was going and he had not asked; he was too involved in the robbery he was planning, but now with his wife scolding him and mentioning his brother, a thing she had never done before, he put her disappearance and the newspaper open at the page announcing the forthcoming event, together.

35

"You been to see Luke?" he said, grabbing her by the wrist.

"What if I have, you ---" She never finished her sentence as his fist hit her in the face and closed her eye. He then threw her on the floor and kicked her several times. She lay in a huddled up state praying for him to go away. The rain of kicks eventually stopped and she felt relieved as she heard the downstairs door slam behind him.

Slowly she raised herself up onto the bed and lay looking at the ceiling dreaming of her Luke, now alive, but for all it mattered, could be dead. Never could she leave her husband; she had promised in the sight of God to love, honour and obey him until death did them part. To her, these vows were sacred; if she had made a mistake, she had to live with it.

***

The police called the following day to see her husband; they showed a lot of interest in her physical appearance. How had she got the black eye, the swelling to her face, the bruises on her arms? They asked if she was all right. Where was her husband? They wished to have words with him over an important matter. He was not in, she truthfully told them. She had not seen him since she had come in last night. No matter, they would find him, of that they were sure.

***

Three days later the postman dropped a letter through Luke's door. Luke studied it a letter to him, no one knew he lived here he thought and looked at the postmark Liverpool. He studied it wondering whom he knew in the town far to the north. Unable to fathom it out he opened the envelope to disclose a postcard that had six words written across the reverse. 'My life is no longer yours.'

The words did not make sense to him and he turned the envelope over to read the address again. Yes it was to him. He placed the card back and propped it up on the mantelpiece wondering what its message meant.

The next day the postman delivered again through his letterbox. He heard the flap snap shut and put his morning cup of coffee down. Two deliveries in two days and him having only moved into this address a couple of weeks ago. Again he studied the postmark but then realised that the writing was in a woman's hand and from all the letters he had received while at training camp, recognised it as Sarah's. He ripped the envelope to shreds in his excitement to retrieve the neatly folded paper inside.

\*\*\*

'My dear Luke; it is my unpleasant duty.' He stopped. What could she have to say that was unpleasant? He read on, 'to have to inform you that your brother Christopher was found dead yesterday morning. The police are not looking for anyone but have a good idea who did it. He was stabbed in the heart. I am sorry that I am the one to tell you this. I will let you know when the funeral is. Love Sarah.'

\*\*\*

Luke sat down trembling and picked up his cup of coffee. He then let the cup fall to the floor as he remembered yesterday's post. Liverpool now rang a bell. That was the port that Jock was sailing to Canada from. What had it said? 'My life is no longer yours'. Of course the debt was paid. It made sense. He must write to Sarah whose address was on the top of the letter, and find out more.

\*\*\*

She was not slow in answering; he took the letter into his bedroom and sat on the bed.

'Dear Luke. Your brother was found dead in some dark alley way off the main road. A single stab to the heart killed him; the police thought it was a contract killing and connected to a robbery he had committed a few days before. The gang had obviously fallen out, and with what the police knew of his mates and goings ons, did not find his death strange.

The funeral has been arranged for the coming Friday and she hoped that after all she had done and him falling out with his brother those years ago, he would still come.' She even offered to put him up for the night. She signed off with 'Love Sarah.'

\*\*\*

It was not his brother's farewell but the idea of seeing Sarah that found him in the church that morning of the funeral after travelling down on the early morning train. The church's windows were still patched with oilcloth even though it had been two years since the last bomb.

The area that Sarah lived in was the poorest in all of London. Hitler had done them a favour, he thought, as the taxi had dropped him off. Now they, the population, had a chance to rebuild new.

Sarah and Luke were the only two there apart from four women and the vicar conducting the service.

Christopher lay in his cheap pine box on a couple of trestles with a small bunch of flowers adorning the lid, which had iron handles instead of brass. It was a cheap affair, fitting Luke thought to a person who treated a woman like he had.

Sarah's appearance was still evident from the kicking he had given her ten days previously. The service was soon over and four men, who looked more like gangsters than funeral directors, entered the church. The coffin was carried from the church to be interred amid an awfully lot of nice people killed in the war. Luke held Sarah's arm but neither had any emotion towards the body entering the ground.

Together they made their way back to Sarah's. They talked late into the night and. Again Sarah made her mind up in the middle of the night, to leave her home and travel back to the village that both had been born in. Neither would tell anyone the truth of the condition Sarah found herself in; all would think the baby was Luke's.

The only thing Christopher had owned was the old farm everyone thought had been sold. Now Sarah and Luke would make it their home.

***

Two months later, with Sarah now showing, they got wed in her father's church. Sarah, who carried a large bouquet of spring flowers, placed them on her mother's grave outside the church door and they both knelt and said a small prayer over her parents' graves.

The house was renovated with what there was in those days, as all builders and materials were at a premium working in all the big towns and cities repairing and rebuilding the worst bombed areas, but Sarah and Luke were happy.

The child was born and the boy grew into a fine little fellow. Christopher's killer was never found and Luke had to live with the fact that he knew but dare not tell anyone.

The moment Sarah's letter announcing his brother's death had arrived, he had burned the envelope and postcard from Liverpool, so destroying all evidence, but it preyed on his conscience, and every morning as he sat at the breakfast table alongside his love, his brother's face stared at him over his son's bowl of porridge.

Even Sarah in the privacy of their own bedroom, admitted that young Robin looked like his father.

\*\*\*

There were few people in Britain that did not know of the 1951 great exhibition held in London to celebrate the commonwealth. They came from all over the world to exhibit their achievements. Sarah and John celebrated their fifth wedding anniversary. Their son had his fifth birthday and the daughter, Sarah, had given birth to a year later became fourth of the family.

*\*\**

Ever since moving back to the village and getting their home habitable, Sarah had taken guests in doing bed and breakfast. There was a roaring trade then from all the hitchhikers and couples on bicycles out for the weekend. The business had grown, as had their children. Luke worked hard on the farm two days a week and the rest of his time he laboured for the farmer next door, who ran a large herd of dairy cows. Milk was something that Luke knew all about.

It was Sarah's trade in bed and breakfast that grew and expanded. The pair had to turn a lot of folk away. Property was cheap and an old house was on the market half a mile from the farm. The day it came on the market Sarah took the two kids into the village, more to have another look around the house than with any idea of purchasing the old Victorian pile?

The place had been empty for over a year and the children found it very dark and spooky with all the downstairs rooms lined in wooden panel walls. Sarah was more interested in a couple of the rooms upstairs. The largest that still held an old iron bed frame made her cry. This was the very place her mother had laid before she died. The little room that her daughter, Eve, said she liked, Sarah told her had once been her very own when she had met her father.

Even at her age, Eve showed a keen interest in her family tree, wanting to know everything there was to know. Her older brother Robin was into electronic things, always fiddling with wires and batteries. He even had to play around with the electric doorbell and once fused all the lights in the house while his mother had six guests in the dining room one day.

Sarah spent over an hour roaming around all the rooms in the old vicarage while the children got bored and pleaded to go home.

*\*\**

Luke arrived home from work that night and had to listen to the children tell him all about the large old house next to the church that their mother had taken them to. Sarah sat beside the fire on the rug and looked on. The two children sitting either side of the fire that winter's night, with Sarah on the rug hogging all the heat, reminded him so much of the time he came home from the estuary, with the five duck that he gave her parents a couple of. That night his mother had sat in front of the fire and shouted at him to dry the dog. How the old brain thinks of times and little things trigger the memory. He thought that the trip today obviously must have meant a lot to Sarah for she lovingly looked at each child as they told father all about the rooms. Sarah said nothing, only her facial expressions showed with pride. All those nights and expectations of how her life was going to be so happy with her young man; then the disappointment as he had to leave her to go off to fight. The children told all to their dad and then looked at mum, now lost in her memories of the sad times; Luke's report of missing in action; her father's death; then those years with his brother. The thought of him made her start and she looked at Luke beaming at her.

"So, have been to the old home have we? And what's the verdict? Are we buying it?" Sarah got to her feet and the pair hugged, to the on-looking amazement of the children. Unknown to Sarah, Luke had heard the old vicarage was coming onto the market and Sarah's dream, ever since the first person had stayed a night in the spare room and paid on leaving, was off owning a hotel.

*\*\**

Luke's boss, whose wife had told him about the sale, was fired with his suggestion of turning it into a hotel. She ran a campsite on the farm and the people staying there had always said what a beautiful coastline it was and if only there was a place to stay other than in a tent. Now an awful lot of those same people had family and would love to return for a week but were too old to sleep under canvas. Sarah was amazed that her husband knew her old home was coming onto the market and had not told her. He explained

41

that he had a good reason not to tell her as only today Pamela, his boss's wife, had put a bid in for the place and he was hoping to go in partnership with her to run it as a hotel.

"And you Sarah are not only to have my half share in the property but are to run it as you please."

Sarah did not know what to make of his proposal, planning and plotting with another woman behind her back but she forgave him that night in bed when he told her that it was going to be hard for all of them the first two or three years. She was glad though to think that she was going home.

The farm and old draughty house they now lived in was going to be bought by his boss and incorporated into the large farm next door. Pamela would only be putting in what they needed so if they took things easy for the first few years, she would need to have a very small part. To Luke's thinking, the asking price was reasonable.

The farm was valued and to his amazement with what work he had done over the last ten years in building up the herd, the price was more than the old vicarage. Pamela and her husband were satisfied that the price was right and Pamela would only need to stake them for a small share until things were got on their feet.

The twelve-roomed hotel was a success from the day it opened. The village had developed in the sixties into a holiday resort and they where there at the beginning.

***

One day in the winter Robin and his sister were looking something up on his computer about the last war for her homework project. Robin stopped on the page displaying the forgotten army. The regiments that boarded each ship home were recorded on other pages and when Eve had learned all she needed for her schoolwork, Robin started to surf the pages looking for his father. From there he went into the births, deaths and marriages genealogy site. Bringing up his father's name proved difficult; he kept getting Christopher Malpass, married to a Sarah Bishop of the address they lived at years ago and Sarah from the very vicarage he now sat in! It intrigued him so much that he went and knocked on his sister's bedroom door.

"Come and look at this!"

Between them they printed off the relevant documents, then found their father's marriage to a Sarah Bishop. Eve said it was too much of a coincidence that the two men from the same village had married different girls with the same name. The only way for that to happen was that she must have married twice. In that case why had neither parent told them that their mother had been married before? The search was now on by them both, to find out the marriage to her first husband and if he was related to them. They found Christopher's death certificate and the date instantly confirmed when compared with his fathers demob papers that gave the date of his return to Britain from Burma that there was no way Luke could be his father, Eve and Robin looked at each other.

"At least we have the same name and mother," she said and gave him a hug, "but who was Christopher I have never heard of him."

"Your fathers brother of course, dad and mum have never told us of him"

"Mum married his brother, what a strange set up."

"But why have they never told us, there must be a good reason."

\*\*\*

At nine that night with the information they had accumulated they went down stairs to ask their parents. Sarah and Luke were looking over the breakfast menu for tomorrow morning. The two kids looked at each other.

"Who's going to tell them we know?" Robin said.

"Mum?" Eve said, holding the sheets of paper out that held the damning evidence. "This you?"

Her mother took the paper and screwed her face up.

"Luke! Look at this!" handing the sheet of paper over. "They know. I told you we should have said something a long time ago. Now it's too late," and she started to cry. The whole story came out and Sarah hugged Robin and Luke to her body. Eve felt as if she was left out. Why did her mother feel so much for Robin? She was the baby of the family.

That night they sat up until the early morning but did not let

Robin know of his true father. Later Sarah and Luke in the privacy of their bedroom decided that Robin had to know that Christopher was his true birth father.

"But we never told them I had a brother. What will they think now at their age to suddenly be confronted by an uncle long dead?"

Sarah made it quite clear to Luke that Robin had the right to know. "Well if we do--."

"There is no if," Sarah said in a stiff voice.

"All right but let's not tell them he was a real bad lot, please. With that agreed they put the light out and went to sleep.

***

Morning found Robin begging for more information. Together the previous night his sister and he had worked out that Robin was the son of his father's brother. His appetite for information was insuperable.

Later, with school over for the day, he was on the computer looking up any information there was. That night he studied his father's regimental roll. There he located the Scotsman his father, Luke, had talked about so often when anyone could get him to discuss his time in the war

***

The records of the regiment showed that their father had been mentioned in dispatches for his bravery in a fight with a party of Japs and also for saving the life of one of the company whose name was mentioned, Jock McCampbell. Father had never told either of them about his epic war in Burma, only saying he was mixed up in an English lot and sometimes with men from the Black Watch a tough lot from many parts and had fought in Burma until the bitter end. Robin was fired with interest; Luke was suddenly his hero and he wanted to find out more. The first thing he wanted to know was who this Jock McCampbell was.

The computer worked overtime that night and Robin admitted defeat but he was determined to seek help.

***

At school next day, his teacher told him to try at the local history group. They were good at finding out about families, especially local ones. Robin told him that it was not local living people he was seeking but an old friend of his father's from the Second World War. "Then in that case," he was told, "contact the British Legion," they are excellent in keeping in touch with lost friends that had served together."

***

Wheels were put in motion by the British Legion to find the man. Eve told her mother that dad was a hero and had been very brave in his time. Sarah told her it was a long time ago and to forget it. Luke, for some reason, did not like speaking of it.

Robin learned a month later that over one hundred Jock McCampbells had enlisted and ten of those had served overseas in the Far East. Of the ten, four had been killed and two had died since. Of the four survivors one had emigrated to Australia and one to Canada. The remaining two lived in Scotland. Robin showed his sister the letter telling him the facts. Surely the two in Scotland would be easy to find?

***

Visiting the local dignitary that ran the local branch of the Legion, Eve and Robin learned that the easiest way to find them was to contact the regiment they were with and see if they held any information of a club as a lot of them had joined the Burma Star Association. The letter arrived at their house a week later and Sarah, shuffling the morning's post out, saw the buff envelope bearing the regiment crest swallowed hard and was Gob smacked, she re-read the name. It was for Robin. What did they want with her son? Taking the letters into the kitchen, she showed it to Luke. He sat up in his chair where he had been leaning on the table reading the paper.

"Give that here dear. What's the silly little bugger playing at writing to them?"

Neither child had mentioned that they were trying to trace Jock. Both had the notion that perhaps they could get a reunion arranged and surprise there father. Luke picked his breakfast knife up to slit the letter open but Sarah implored him to show some consideration towards their son.

45

"He never opens our mail; leave his alone."

"Ok, but I want to know what's going on."

Neither kid would let on to their parents that evening after school. It was private, they told them.

The two addresses proved that neither knew their father.

*** 

The search spread wider a month later. The address of the man in Australia was produced. Letters were exchanged but the old man had no knowledge of Luke. He had spent all his time in the catering corps and never saw any action. The trail seemed to die out, but Robin never gave up hope that someone knew of this red headed Scotsman.

Luke was relived when Eve told her mother that she had given up all hope of finding the man and the possibility of uniting him with father. Sarah told her that in her opinion, she or Robin would never find him.

*** 

All her life with Luke since he had come home from the war, he had never spoken of the Scotsman but could not figure it out as now Luke knowing of his kids trying to find the man was giving him many sleepless nights.

*** 

From the time they had both started to search for Jock, a full year had passed and neither child was looking any more. Sarah picked the letter up from the doormat early. The Canadian stamp immediately drew her attention to the name, Robin Malpass,' turning the envelope over she saw the name of the sender Mc Cambell taking it to the kitchen she showed it to Luke.

"It's from Jock. It must be! Robin has found him." Luke went a shade of white and Sarah put her arm around him to comfort him from the shock.

"My God!" he said. "What the hell is he playing at?" Sarah was mystified by Luke's reactions. "You don't know the truth," he said, and Sarah pulled a chair up closer to him.

"No, you had better tell me. You never saved his life, did you? It was a story to get drinks from the others."

"It certainly was not! It is true, but it's what happened before he left this country. I need a drink!" he said. He got up and went to the side cupboard and extracted a bottle of gin. Sitting down, he poured a teacup full and his hand was shaking so much he spilt the liquid over the table and took a couple of large swigs. Sarah looked on speechless. Never before had she seen Luke behave like this.

"Whatever is the matter?" Luke took her hand in his and squeezed it.

"Sarah; don't tell Robin for heavens sake; it could destroy all he now thinks of his Scotsman. Let the boy imagine what he likes but never tell him his Jock is a murderer." Sarah snatched her hand away from Luke's and gazed at him.

"A murderer! Who did he kill?

"Christopher of course!"

"Christopher? Why?"

"Because he knew I loved you and he owed his life to me, he wrote to me telling me 'he no longer owed his life to me' and the next day your letter came telling me of his death.' Tears were running down his face as Sarah tried to console him.

"I agree Robin must never know and you have to forget all about it.

The ringing of the alarm clock up in Eve's room made the pair pull themselves together. "Don't say a thing Luke," Sarah said. "Let's play this quietly."

***

Robin and Eve entered the kitchen together and Sarah handed the letter to her son. Eve immediately jumped up from her chair to lie over Robin's shoulder as he opened the envelope. An official looking letter was pulled out and Robin read it. Luke held his breath as Robin looked at him and said,

"It's about Jock Mc'Campbell who fought with you in Burma. He's dead."

The gasp Luke gave out was audible to all present.

"Dead! You sure? He was three years younger than me."

"It says here he's dead, look dad."

Luke took the offered sheet of paper and together Sarah and he read it. It was from Luke's son in Canada, who had seen Robins web site on his computer. He was sorry to tell Robin that his father had been killed in a gunfight in a town four hundred miles west of Montreal while trying to rob a bank.

Eve thought it very disrespectful of the parents smiling at the news.

*END*